PUFFIN BOOKS

MARY KATE AND
THE SCHOOL BUS

Mary Kate was five. She had been five for a whole week now, and tomorrow she would be going to school! She already knew the faces of some of the children, because when she was little she used to wave from the window when they went by in the school bus, but now she was big she would be going in that bus herself. All her school things, her new sandals and plimsolls, and her beautiful new satchel with her painting pinny and pencil sharpener in it, were waiting in her bedroom, and it wouldn't be long now before she was using them.

'My goodness, Mary Kate,' said Granny next morning, 'You *do* look smart. And so grown up,' and then Mary Kate went skipping down the road ahead of Mummy to her very first day at school. And it was all so interesting and so very busy, what with the nice elephant picture over her new coat peg, playing in the playhouse, and making a picture to take home to Mummy, not to mention eating such a big dinner, that it wasn't so very surprising that when storytime came Mary Kate was fast asleep on the floor, and quite missed the story!

Many children who already know Helen Morgan's gentle, homely stories about Mary Kate from her other Young Puffin books, *Meet Mary Kate* and *Mary Kate and the Jumble Bear*, will be pleased to hear more about her in this book, and these stories will of course be specially interesting and reassuring to any child who is about to start school and wondering what it will be like, or who is still finding kindergarten a new experience.

HELEN MORGAN

MARY KATE AND
THE SCHOOL BUS

and Other Stories

ILLUSTRATED BY

SHIRLEY HUGHES

PUFFIN BOOKS

in association with Faber and Faber

Puffin Books, Penguin Books Ltd, Harmondsworth, Middlesex, England
Viking Penguin Inc., 40 West 23rd Street, New York, New York 10010, U.S.A.
Penguin Books Australia Ltd, Ringwood, Victoria, Australia
Penguin Books Canada Limited, 2801 John Street, Markham, Ontario, Canada L3R 1B4
Penguin Books (N.Z.) Ltd, 182–190 Wairau Road, Auckland 10, New Zealand

—

First published by Faber and Faber 1970
Published in Puffin Books 1977
Reprinted 1979, 1982, 1985, 1987

—

—

Printed and bound in Great Britain by
Cox & Wyman Ltd, Reading
Set in Monotype Bembo

CONTENTS

MARY KATE AND THE SCHOOL BUS   7

MARY KATE GOES TO SCHOOL   17

A NAME AND AN ELEPHANT   28

THE FAIRY TOOTH   38

A SPOT OF BOTHER   48

A WALK AND AUNT MARY   58

THE SCHOOL SPORTS   70

MARY KATE AND THE
SCHOOL BUS

IT was snowing. Mary Kate stood at the front window, watching the big flakes falling in the strange, unhurried way of snow beginning. Now they came straight down, now they turned and twisted and drifted sideways. The snow that fell on the road and on the front steps of the house melted at once. On the spiky plants of the rockery, though, the white flakes settled like sudden winter flowers.

A long, low green bus was coming up the hill. It was taking the older boys and girls from the village to the schools in the nearby town. At the same time a small blue bus was coming *down* the hill. It was the bus that collected the younger children from the country cottages and took them a roundabout way to the village school.

'I shall go on that bus when I go to school, shan't I, Mummy?' said Mary Kate. She had said it so many times before that Mummy didn't even bother to answer. All the same, she looked out to see the bus go by – and it was then she noticed it was snowing.

Mary Kate had said it was, but Mummy hadn't been listening.

'What a nuisance!' cried Mummy. 'I hope it's not going to last. We had enough of it at Christmas. I thought we'd finished with snow for this winter.'

She flicked her duster rather crossly round the room and then went upstairs to make the beds.

Mary Kate pressed her nose against the cold window-pane. She had been hoping the snow *would* last because she wanted Daddy to help her make a snowman. They had made a lovely one at Christmas.

The snow was falling faster now. There was a scattering of white flakes on the front steps and the rockery was all over snow-flowers.

By lunchtime the snow was quite thick but the steps were clear. Mummy had swept them. She banged the broom hard against the wall to show how annoyed she was.

'We *must* go to Granny's,' she said. 'I promised to do some shopping for her this afternoon. She's got such a nasty chesty cough she can't possibly go out.'

Mary Kate was delighted to hear they were going out in the snow but she put on a worried face and said

'Oh, dear!' because she could see Mummy didn't want to go.

After lunch Mummy dressed Mary Kate in her warm trousers over her skirt and her long boots over her trousers. She had to wear two pairs of socks because the boots were a bit too big.

Mummy pulled Mary Kate's hat well down over her ears, wound her scarf twice round her neck and tucked the tops of her mittens into the sleeves of her coat.

'There,' she said. 'You'll do.'

Mary Kate didn't feel as though she would do at all. She felt so bundled up she didn't think she could move. She could, though. She plodded down the front steps holding Mummy's hand, which she couldn't feel because of her thick mittens and Mummy's furry gloves.

When they reached the front gate they saw that no one had walked along the narrow footpath since the snow started that morning. The snow was clean and beautiful, just waiting for Mary Kate to mark it.

She put her feet down slowly and carefully, watching her big boots sink deep into the snow. She thought she was walking straight but when she looked over her shoulder she saw her footprints following her all wiggly. Mummy's footprints were wiggly, too, and

rather smudgy. She wasn't walking as carefully as
Mary Kate.

They caught the bus to the village. It had stopped
snowing while they were having lunch but by the time
they got off the bus it had started again.

'I hope this doesn't keep on all afternoon,' Mummy
said, but it did.

By three o'clock the snow was really deep. It looked
so chilly outside that even Mary Kate didn't want to

leave Granny's cosy little parlour and set out for home.

'I meant to catch the ten to four bus,' said Mummy, anxiously watching the fast falling snow. 'I wonder how long we shall have to wait for it? It's sure to be running late.'

'Why don't you go up early and get a lift on the school bus?' suggested Granny. 'Mr Beadle is very obliging. He doesn't mind giving the mothers a lift when they come to meet the children in bad weather.'

'I think we will,' Mummy said. 'After all, he passes the door. Get your things, Mary Kate. We'll warm them by the fire so you can start out nice and comfortable.'

Mr Beadle didn't in the least mind giving Mummy and Mary Kate a lift in his little blue bus. There was plenty of room. Mary Kate thought it was lovely to be on the school bus at last but she was glad Mummy was with her. She didn't really know any of the children even though some of them waved to her whenever they saw her standing in the window or at the front gate, waiting for the bus to go by.

The bus climbed slowly up the hill towards Mary Kate's house. A huge lorry, with a long trailer loaded with wood, was coming down the hill. Suddenly the lorry skidded, swung sideways across the road and stopped with its front stuck in the hedge. The trailer swung round, too, and the tail of it crashed through the hedge on the other side of the road.

All the children cried out when they saw the lorry skid. Mr Beadle pulled the bus well over to the side of the road and stopped. Then he climbed out and went, as fast as he could, up the hill towards the lorry, but before he reached it the lorry driver was out on the road, wiping his forehead with his handkerchief and looking at the mess.

'Thank goodness the driver wasn't hurt,' Mummy said, when she saw he was all right. 'And thank goodness it didn't happen a few yards higher up. He'd have crashed into our front garden.'

The next few moments were busy ones. Several cars and vans came up the hill behind Mr Beadle's bus. They had to stop, of course. One of them drove across to the other side of the road, reversed in a gateway and went back to the village. Then Mr Turner, the policeman, arrived on his scooter and Mr Beadle came back to the bus and said the breakdown truck had been sent for but he didn't know how long it would be.

'It looks as if we're in for a long wait,' Mummy said. 'And we're so near home, too. I wonder if we could get by? Come on, Mary Kate, let's try.'

So Mummy and Mary Kate got out of the bus and went up the hill to where the lorry was.

It was no use. They saw that they couldn't possibly squeeze themselves between the lorry and the hedge. Nor could they get between the lorry and the trailer, even if they ducked down low.

The long, low green bus appeared on the other side of the lorry. Here was another load of school children who were going to be late for their teas.

The driver of the green bus came to talk to the lorry driver. So did Mr Beadle. They said that if the lorry driver could move back just a little bit the children could change over buses.

'I can take my lot home in Mr Beadle's bus and he can take his lot in mine,' said the driver of the green bus.

'Sorry, mate,' the lorry driver said. 'I can't shift her. I've tried. She's wedged right up against the trailer and the wheels just spin round in this snow.'

He looked at Mummy and Mary Kate, who were standing there shivering and wondering if they could get into their back garden by way of the field. They were so near, it seemed silly not to be able to get into the house.

'You and the kiddy had best get up in my cab, lady,' said the lorry driver. 'You'll freeze out here.'

Mary Kate felt that her feet were freezing already, in spite of the two pairs of socks. She was very glad indeed to be lifted up into the high cab of the lorry, out of the way of the wind and the stinging snow.

She and Mummy had hardly settled themselves in the seats when Mummy gave a funny little screech.

'What an idiot I am!' she cried. 'All we have to do is get down the other side.'

She leaned across Mary Kate and opened the door. Mary Kate made herself small while Mummy squeezed past her and in another moment she was being lifted out of the lorry and put down on the footpath outside her own front gate.

'Thanks very much,' called Mummy to the lorry driver.

The lorry driver stared at the empty cab. So did the driver of the green bus. Then they started to laugh.

'Thanks, lady,' shouted the driver of the green bus as Mummy put her key into the front door. 'You must think we're a bright lot.'

Mummy and Mary Kate couldn't imagine what he meant but it wasn't long before they knew.

They stood in the front window watching the children from the green bus climb through the cab of the lorry and straggle down the hill towards Mr

Beadle's bus. Then little children from Mr Beadle's bus came up the hill and were lifted through the cab and helped into the green bus. In a little while both buses had been turned round and all the children were on their way home. Some of the big boys and girls were walking because Mr Beadle's bus was too small to take them all.

It was dark before the lorry and trailer were set straight on the road again. It took a long time to do, and a lot of tea and a great plate of sandwiches went out to the lorry driver before it was done. Mary Kate watched it all, eating her tea at the little table in the window.

She was sorry when the lorry driver waved good-bye to her and drove away. She had been half hoping Daddy would have to climb through the cab when he came up the hill from the station.

MARY KATE GOES TO SCHOOL

MARY KATE was five. She had been five for a whole week and tomorrow she would be going to school.

'You must have your hair washed this morning,' Mummy said, while they were having breakfast.

Mary Kate put on a scowly face. She didn't like having her hair washed.

Mummy pretended not to see the scowl. 'Granny said she might look in this afternoon,' she said.

Mary Kate brightened up a bit. 'I hope she does,' she said. 'Then I can show her all my school things.'

Mummy had put all Mary Kate's school things on the little blue dressing-table in her bedroom, ready for the morning. Mary Kate went upstairs straight after breakfast to have another look at them.

First she looked at her new sandals. Her old ones didn't fit her any more. They had gone to a jumble sale. Next to the sandals was a pair of brown strap shoes. Mary Kate could do them up all by herself. She couldn't tie shoelaces properly yet. She tied them all loose and tangly so that her shoes fell off when she hurried or the laces came undone and tripped her up.

Next to the shoes was a pair of black plimsolls. Mary Kate had never had plimsolls before because she had never needed them. She picked them up and sniffed at their strange, rubbery smell. Then she stretched the elastic front of one of them, to see it spring back into shape.

Mummy had been to several shops to find the elastic-fronted plimsolls. 'You'll be a nuisance to your teacher if you have lace-up ones,' she had said.

That was really how Mary Kate had come by the strap shoes. 'Shan't I be a nuisance with my shoes?' she had asked, looking down at her brown lace-ups.

So Mummy bought her new shoes and Granny bought her three pairs of short white socks. When they arrived home with all the shoes and socks, they found a parcel in the back porch. It was from Aunt Mary and inside it was a school satchel.

'This is to carry all your bits and pieces to school,' said the card that was with the satchel.

'What bits and pieces?' asked Mary Kate.

'All sorts of things,' Mummy told her. 'You'll see.'

One of the bits and pieces arrived the very next day. It came from Auntie Dot and Uncle Ned. It was a bright red pencil case. Inside it was a little ruler, a rainbow-coloured pencil with a rubber on the end, a blue pencil without a rubber and a rubber without a pencil.

'You'll need a pencil sharpener,' Daddy said, when he saw the pencil case, so he bought her one.

Mary Kate was very pleased. She had never had so many new things before, except at Christmas or on her birthday.

Now all the things were on her dressing-table and tomorrow she would put on her brown pleated skirt and a shirt blouse and wear her new white socks and her strap shoes. She touched the toe of the left shoe with the tip of her finger and then rubbed the place quickly with her handkerchief so as not to leave a mark on the shiny brown leather.

When Granny came that afternoon, she brought two more surprises for Mary Kate. The first was a box of coloured pencils from Uncle Jack and the second was a painting pinny, which Granny had made.

It was green with a pattern of tiny squares and squiggles all over it. 'I thought it was just the right sort of pattern for a painting pinny,' Granny said. 'A few more spots and splashes will hardly show. And it doesn't matter which way round you wear it because

it's just one long piece of stuff with a hole in the middle for your head. The girdle is sewn on quite firmly, all you have to do is tie it round your waist.'

She slipped the pinny over Mary Kate's head, to see if it fitted her. It did.

Mary Kate pulled the pinny off again, rumpling her newly-washed hair. As she gave it to Granny to fold she caught sight of a strip of white tape with writing on it.

'What does that say?' she asked, turning the pinny round to look.

'It says MARY WILLIAMS,' Granny told her. She looked across at Mummy. 'Haven't you taught the child to recognize her own name yet?' she asked.

'Of course I have,' Mummy said, 'but not like that.' She took her shopping pad and pencil from the kitchen cabinet. 'Write your name for Granny,' she said.

So Mary Kate sat down at the table and wrote her name. She wrote it slowly and carefully in big, round, wobbly letters – MARY KATE WILLIAMS. The E and the S were back to front, but it was quite easy to read.

'That's very good,' nodded Granny, when she saw it. 'I'm sorry I didn't put KATE on your pinny. Never mind, you'll know it's yours, won't you?'

The next morning Mary Kate was down in the dining-room before Daddy had even started his breakfast.

'My word, you're early this morning,' he said.

'I'm going to school today,' said Mary Kate.

'So you are!' cried Daddy, pretending he had forgotten. 'Well, you'd better come and eat a hearty breakfast. You'll need to keep your strength up. Here, have one of my eggs.'

So Mary Kate had one of Daddy's boiled eggs and Mummy put another one in the saucepan for him and an extra one in case Mary Kate felt like eating two.

'Bread and butter?' asked Daddy, cutting a slice into fingers. He called them soldiers. He said the little crusty one at the end was the sergeant.

As soon as Daddy had gone, Mummy and Mary Kate went upstairs to get dressed.

Mary Kate fastened her shoes herself, just to show Mummy that she could. When she was dressed, she looked very smart – except for her hair, which was all night-wild and anyhow.

Mummy brushed out the tangles and tied the hair back with a ribbon.

'There!' said Mummy. 'You'll do.'

Mary Kate looked at herself in the mirror and thought she didn't look like Mary Kate at all. It was very odd. She didn't even *feel* like Mary Kate this morning.

'Are we going on the school bus?' she asked, as Mummy helped her into her coat.

'Not this morning,' Mummy said. 'We'll walk across the field. We've plenty of time. We'll get there nice and early, so you can find your way about a bit before school starts.'

So they went out the back way. Mummy had to push Jacky back into the kitchen and shut the door quickly, because he wanted to go with them. They could hear him barking as they went down the garden and through the gate into the wood. There were primroses growing by the path. Mary Kate would have liked to pick some but Mummy told her not to stop today.

So she hurried after Mummy along the path to the stile and across the field to the little bridge. There they stopped for a moment, because the ducks were coming.

'No bread today, ducks,' called Mary Kate. 'I'm going to school.'

The ducks took no notice of her. They just swam under the bridge and away round the bend in the stream.

Mummy and Mary Kate went on across the field. When they came to the kissing-gate, Mary Kate ran through first and held the gate shut.

'Pay me! Pay me!' she cried, so Mummy paid her a kiss to make her open the gate.

The weedy footpath behind the churchyard was too narrow for them to walk along side by side, so Mary Kate trotted along behind, taking care not to tread on

Mummy's heels. Mummy wiggled the latch of the gate in the churchyard wall and they went through the churchyard and out into the village street.

There was the school, a little way beyond the church – and there were the school children, in ones and twos, dawdling into the playground.

Mary Kate began to feel a bit funny inside. She held Mummy's hand now, very tightly.

Mummy looked across the road towards the little lane where Granny lived.

'Good gracious me,' she cried. 'There's Granny, standing at her gate. Look, she's seen us. She's waving. Wave to her, Mary Kate.'

So Mary Kate waved to Granny. She jumped up and down and waved so hard that her satchel bumped about and banged her on the back.

'Let's go and have a quick word with her,' suggested Mummy. 'We've got time.'

'My goodness, Mary Kate,' said Granny, when they reached her cottage. 'You *do* look smart. And so grown-up.' She put her hand into her pocket and pulled out a little packet.

'Here's something else to put in your satchel,' she said. 'Biscuits. In case you feel peckish when you have your mid-morning milk.'

'Thank you,' said Mary Kate. She swung her satchel round to the front and unbuckled it and put the biscuits inside. Mummy had already told her about the mid-morning milk. She was looking forward to having a little bottle all to herself and a straw to drink through.

They said good-bye to Granny and Mary Kate went off down the lane a little way ahead of Mummy, feeling quite happy. She turned and waved to Granny just once more before she and Mummy crossed the road. Then she let go Mummy's hand and skipped along the path towards the open gate of the playground, just as Uncle Jack and Uncle Ned, Auntie Mary and Mummy had done, when they were children.

A NAME AND AN ELEPHANT

MARY KATE was following Mummy and Mummy was following Miss Chesney. Miss Chesney was the Headmistress. Mummy and Mary Kate had been in her office answering questions while she filled in a form. Now she was taking them to see Mary Kate's classroom and meet her teacher.

The classroom had big windows, set high in the wall. Through one of them Mary Kate could see the top of a tree and a patch of sky and through the other she could see the church tower. All round the walls were paintings and drawings and big coloured diagrams and pictures. In one corner was a doll's house and a cot with a doll in it and in another corner was a table piled with books. There was a stove with a huge fireguard round it and, most wonderful of all, there was a little playhouse, with windows and a door and real curtains. Mary Kate wanted to run across the room and peep inside it but Miss Chesney was speaking to someone who had just come in.

'Ah, there you are, Miss Laurie,' she was saying. 'We have a new pupil this morning.' She put her hand on Mary Kate's shoulder. 'This is Mary Kate,' she said, 'and this is her mother. Mrs Williams, this is Miss Laurie. She will be Mary Kate's teacher.'

'How do you do,' said Mummy and Miss Laurie together, and then Miss Laurie said, 'Hallo, Mary Kate. I'm so glad you've come to join us. The others will be in soon. Would you like to have a quick look round before they come, then I'll show you where to put your coat.'

Off went Mary Kate, to look in the playhouse. Inside were two tiny chairs and a little table, a small set of shelves on a box, painted to look like a dresser, and a bushel box on end, painted to look like a cooker. On the dresser were dolly pots and pans and cups and saucers and plates.

Mary Kate just stood there, looking and looking and thinking what marvellous games she could have in the little house, with Teddy and Black Bobo and Dorabella and Og, the Golly. Then she remembered that they were all at home, still tucked in their beds, while she was at school.

'Mary Kate,' said Miss Laurie's voice. The door of the little house opened and the teacher looked in.

29

'Mummy's going now,' she said. 'Come and say good-bye to her and I'll show you where to put your things.'

Mary Kate followed Miss Laurie and Mummy out of the classroom into the cloakroom. There were pegs low down all round the wall and two little low-down washbasins. Everything was just the right height for Mary Kate.

'Good-bye, pet,' Mummy said, giving her a quick kiss. 'I'll come and fetch you after school.'

'This will be your peg,' said Miss Laurie, almost before Mary Kate had time to say good-bye to Mummy. 'Let me help you with your coat.'

Mary Kate looked at the peg. It had a picture of a red elephant just above it.

'Do you know what this picture is?' asked Miss Laurie, hanging Mary Kate's coat on the peg and putting her hat on top.

'Elephant,' said Mary Kate and then she saw that all the pegs had pictures and they were all different. The other pegs had names, too, but Mary Kate's didn't.

'Good,' smiled Miss Laurie. 'Now you just remember that your hat and coat are hanging under the red elephant and you won't lose them. I'll print

out a name for you in a moment, but I'll find you a place in the classroom, first.'

She showed Mary Kate a little table and chair. 'You can sit here,' she said. 'There's a drawer to put your things in and this is so you won't forget where you are.'

She took a card out of a box and fixed it firmly to a corner of the table with four big drawing pins. It was a picture of a red elephant, just like the one in the cloakroom.

'Now I'll just get a card for your name,' said Miss Laurie, looking in another box. 'Then I'll go and ring the bell and let the others in. Now, what shall I put on this card? What do they call you at home?'

'Mary Kate,' said Mary Kate, surprised, wondering what else they could call her.

'Right,' said Miss Laurie. 'That's what we'll call you, then. That way we shan't muddle you up with the other Mary.'

Mary Kate said nothing. She wasn't sure she liked the idea of another Mary.

Miss Laurie went out of the room and a moment later Mary Kate heard the clanging of a bell close by. The noise was so loud she had to put her hands over her ears to shut it out.

Then the children came in, talking and laughing and

32

pushing at one another, struggling to hang up their hats and coats. Mary Kate could see them through the open door of the classroom. There seemed to be a great many of them. She hoped they weren't *all* coming in, but they were.

They clattered into the classroom and made their way to their places, all staring at Mary Kate as they passed her. Some carried satchels, some carried books and some had dolls and teddy bears.

Mary Kate wished she had brought her Teddy to school with her – or even Og, the Golly.

A little girl with a long, fair pigtail came and stood next to Mary Kate. Mary Kate had a feeling she had seen her before, somewhere, but she couldn't think where.

'You've come, then,' said the little girl. 'What's your name?'

Mary Kate told her.

'I'm Susan,' said the little girl. 'Susan Bates.' She nodded towards another little girl with untidy dark hair falling about her face. 'That's Jane. She lives next door to me.'

Then Mary Kate knew where she had seen Susan before. She and Jane were two of the children who travelled on the school bus. They had often waved to Mary Kate as she stood at the front gate.

A boy in a green jersey came and stood by Susan. 'Who's she?' he asked, nodding towards Mary Kate.

'Mary Kate,' said Susan. 'She's new.'

Mary Kate felt very new indeed as she watched the children go to their places and show one another the things they had brought to school. Then Miss Laurie rapped on her desk for silence and began to call the register.

When Miss Laurie said 'MARY TURNER,' Mary Kate stared at the little girl who answered. She had short fair hair, held back with a blue Alice band. Mary Kate didn't think she looked in the least bit like another Mary.

She was so busy thinking about it that she didn't hear Miss Laurie call her name. Susan had to nudge her, to make her answer.

'You're the last one,' said Susan. 'Valerie Watson used to be last, but now you are.'

Mary Kate liked being the last name on the register. It made her feel special.

'Susan,' called Miss Laurie, 'show Mary Kate the doll's house and all the other things. Perhaps you'd like to play house with her, for a while.'

So Susan took the doll out of its cot and Mary Kate dressed it and sat it on a chair in the little house, and they played a marvellous game, with Mary Kate being mother and Susan being father and the milkman and the baker and the district nurse, who had to come because the doll baby was ill.

In the middle of the morning all the children had a little bottle of milk, just as Mummy said they would. Mary Kate bent her straw and Miss Laurie gave her another one. Susan helped her eat the biscuits Granny

had given her and then they both went out into the playground to run about till the bell went.

After playtime, Miss Laurie gave Mary Kate some wax crayons and a huge sheet of paper and told her to draw a picture to take home to Mummy. She drew the playhouse.

When the bell rang again, Mary Kate thought it must be time to go home, but Susan said it wasn't.

'We haven't had our dinner yet,' she said. 'Don't you want any?'

Mary Kate *did* want her dinner. She ate it all and then she had two helpings of apricots and rice. Afterwards, Susan tried to teach her to skip but Mary Kate kept tripping over the rope, so they played 'higher and higher' with some of the other children.

In the afternoon Miss Laurie read a story to the class, but Mary Kate didn't hear much of it. She was fast asleep on the floor by the doll's house.

When she woke up the children were singing.

'This old man,' they yelled, 'He played one...'

Mary Kate knew that song because Granny sang it to her, so she joined in and yelled with the others.

Then it really *was* time to go home. Mary Kate rushed into the cloakroom with Susan and there was Mummy, standing by the door.

Mary Kate ran to her and hugged her. 'I drew you a picture,' she said, 'and I cut a blue cat out of sticky paper and I went in the playhouse and I played with the doll and I had two puddings and Susan taught me how to play "higher and higher". That's Susan, over there, with the long hair. She's my best friend. She says I can sit next to her on the school bus tomorrow. Can I, Mummy?'

'We'll see,' smiled Mummy. 'Which is your peg?'

'The one with the elephant,' Mary Kate told her, but when she looked at the elephant she saw that Miss Laurie had put a card with her name on above it.

MARY KATE WILLIAMS, she had written, in big, round, red writing.

'That's right,' said Mary Kate, touching the card with her fingertips. 'That's my name. Mummy, did you know there's another Mary? She's in my class . . .'

'Is she?' said Mummy, picking Mary Kate's hat up from the floor. 'Never mind. There's only one Mary Kate.'

Mary Kate buttoned her coat up crooked. 'Tomorrow I'm going to be father,' she said, 'and Susan's going to be mother. And I'm going to stick my blue cat in a book and write "cat". Susan said I could.'

THE FAIRY TOOTH

MARY KATE had a loose tooth. When she put her tongue behind it, it moved. It was one of her four front teeth so she stood in front of the mirror and pushed at the tooth to see if she could see it moving. She couldn't. It wasn't loose enough for that.

'My tooth moves,' she said, when she went downstairs to breakfast.

'Oh, no!' cried Mummy. 'Let me see.'

'You can't see it,' Mary Kate told her. She made a toothy face at Mummy. 'I can feel it, though. I can move it with my tongue.'

Mummy gave a big sigh. 'Oh, dear, what a pity. I suppose it had to come, but I did hope you wouldn't start losing your teeth just yet.'

Mary Kate was puzzled. 'I haven't lost it,' she said, feeling the tooth with her fingertip, to make sure. 'It's still there.'

'Not for long,' Mummy said. 'They'll all come out,

sooner or later. They're your baby teeth. In a few years they'll all be gone and you'll have your grown-up teeth.'

Mary Kate didn't say anything. She was too busy trying to bite a piece of toast without using her loose tooth. A day or two later, Mummy said, 'How would you like to have lunch and tea with Granny on Saturday?'

'Why?' asked Mary Kate.

'Because Daddy and I want to go into town and do some shopping,' Mummy said.

Mary Kate wanted to know what sort of shopping. Sometimes she liked going shopping and sometimes she didn't.

'Clothes, mostly,' Mummy told her. 'Daddy wants some shirts and socks. And I'd like some summer shoes and at least one cotton dress. We'd like to have a good look round. Granny thought you'd rather stay with her.'

Mary Kate thought so, too. Shirts and socks and shoes were the sort of shopping she didn't like.

'Will Uncle Jack be there?' asked Mary Kate, when she and Mummy and Jacky, the dog, were on their way to Granny's on Saturday morning.

Mary Kate hadn't known her Uncle Jack very long.

He had been travelling round the world ever since she was born and had only come home a few months ago. He still travelled a lot, but not very far now, so he stayed with Granny most week-ends.

'I'm not sure if he'll be home this week or not,' Mummy said. 'Granny didn't say.'

'I hope he is,' Mary Kate said, skipping along the narrow path behind the churchyard. She liked Uncle Jack. He told her marvellous stories about his adventures abroad.

When they reached Granny's cottage, they saw that Uncle Jack *was* there. He was in the yard, chopping firewood. Jacky rushed at him and nearly knocked him over. He liked Uncle Jack, too.

'Hey!' cried Uncle Jack. 'Call off your horrible hound. He's eating me. Why don't you feed him before you bring him out?'

'Down, Jacky,' Mummy said, jerking at the lead.

'*Jacky!*' snorted Uncle Jack. 'Whatever made you call him that?'

'He reminded me of you,' said Mummy. 'He never stayed put for more than five minutes at a time.'

Uncle Jack threw a piece of kindling at her. Mummy ducked and the stick hit the dustbin. Jacky leapt after it, thinking it had been thrown for him to chase. He

crashed into the bin and the lid fell off, with a terrible clatter.

Granny poked her head out of the bathroom window.

'What's all that noise?' she called, but nobody told her. They were all laughing too much to speak.

Mummy gave Mary Kate a bag with her brush and comb and pinafore in it. Then she went home.

'I've a bit of shopping I must do this morning,' Granny said, when she had made the beds. 'I wonder if

I can trust you and Uncle Jack to keep an eye on the lunch for me?'

'No, you can't,' Uncle Jack said, coming in from the yard just in time to hear her. 'But you can trust us to do the shopping. You'll come with me, won't you, Mary Kate?'

'Yes,' said Mary Kate at once. This was going to be the kind of shopping she *did* like.

Granny made out a list of the things she wanted and gave Mary Kate a basket to carry.

'May I buy myself a jammy doughnut for my tea?' asked Uncle Jack, as they went out of the front door.

'Yes,' said Granny, 'and you may buy one for Mary Kate, too.'

Mary Kate trotted happily along beside Uncle Jack, carrying the empty basket. First they went to the Post Office to buy a book of stamps and then they went to the greengrocer's for the fruit and vegetables that Granny wanted.

'Let's buy Granny some flowers,' suggested Uncle Jack. 'What do you think she'd like? Daffodils or anemones?'

'Both,' said Mary Kate, so they bought both.

Uncle Jack put the flowers carefully on top of the basket. 'I'd better carry it now,' he said. 'It's heavy.'

They crossed the road to the Bun Shop and Uncle Jack looked at Granny's list. 'Malt loaf,' he said, 'and a large wholemeal.'

'Don't forget the jammy doughnuts,' Mary Kate reminded him.

'Now we'll go to the Tuck Shop,' said Uncle Jack, when they had bought the bread and cakes. 'I fancy some peanut crunch. How about you?'

'I don't think I can eat it,' Mary Kate told him. 'I've got a loose tooth. It wobbles when I bite something hard.'

'Oh, bad luck,' said Uncle Jack. He bought her some chocolate drops and jelly fruits and then he bought a box of crystallized ginger for Granny.

'That's the lot,' he said, checking with the list. 'Home now.'

Lunch was ready by the time they arrived. Mary Kate helped Granny to set the table while Uncle Jack carved the joint.

There was apple pie and custard for pudding. Mary Kate was half-way through hers when she suddenly made a gurgly noise and put her hand to her mouth.

'There's a hard thing in my pie,' she said. 'It must be a stone.'

She took the hard thing out of her mouth.

'Apples don't have stones,' Granny said. 'Whatever can it be?' She leaned over to have a look.

'Why, it's your tooth!' she cried, when she saw what was in Mary Kate's hand.

'I never knew my tooth looked like that!' said Mary Kate, staring at the tiny, shiny thing.

She put her tongue into the place where the tooth had been. 'How did such a little tooth come out of such a big space?' she asked, wonderingly.

'It isn't really a big space,' Granny told her. 'It just feels big to your tongue.'

'Ah, me!' sighed Uncle Jack, putting on a funny voice, 'Tongues are terrible things for not telling the truth.'

Granny fetched a piece of tissue paper from the kitchen and wrapped Mary Kate's tooth in it.

'Keep it safely tucked in your pocket,' she said. 'You must take it home and put it under your pillow tonight.'

Mary Kate stared at her. 'Whatever for?' she asked. It seemed a very odd thing to do.

Uncle Jack leaned forward and said, solemnly, 'Because it isn't really your tooth, Mary Kate. It belongs to the fairies. They only lend these tiny teeth to you for a little while. Then they want them back.' He wagged his finger at her. 'Make no mistake, Mary Kate. This is a fairy tooth. The fairies will come for it tonight. And they'll leave you something else in its place.'

'What?' asked Mary Kate. She didn't know whether to believe Uncle Jack or not.

'Wait and see,' said Granny, smiling.

That night, when Mummy was putting her to bed, Mary Kate took the tooth out of her pocket.

'Granny said I must put the tooth under my pillow,' she said. 'Uncle Jack said the fairies will come for it and leave me something else instead. They won't really, will they, Mummy?'

Mummy smiled – the same sort of smile that Granny had smiled. 'Wait and see,' she said.

46

In the morning, Mary Kate remembered about the tooth the moment she woke up. She slid her hand under her pillow. The piece of tissue paper was still there.

Feeling rather disappointed, Mary Kate pulled it out and began to unfold it. Long before she reached the hard thing in the middle she knew it couldn't possibly be her tiny fairy tooth. It wasn't. It was a shiny, silvery 5p piece.

A SPOT OF BOTHER

IT was a fine May morning and Mary Kate was up in her bedroom getting ready for school. At least, she should have been getting ready, but she couldn't find her vest. It wasn't on the chair, where it should have been, and it wasn't on the bed. It wasn't even on the floor under the bed, with her yesterday's socks. The socks weren't supposed to be there, so Mary Kate picked them up and took them to the bathroom to put them in the linen basket.

While she was there, she thought she might as well wash. She ran the water and looked for her face cloth. It wasn't on its little hook. It was screwed up in a soggy bundle between the bath taps.

Then Mary Kate remembered she had undressed in the bathroom last night while her bath was running. Mummy had come in and told her to pick her things up off the floor. She had put her blouse in the linen basket because the collar was grubby. Perhaps her vest had been put in there, too. Mary

Kate pulled her yesterday's socks out of the basket again and her yesterday's blouse, but her vest wasn't there. She dried her hands and was back in the bedroom before she remembered she had been going to wash. She trotted back to the bathroom.

Mummy came upstairs just as Mary Kate started to clean her teeth.

'Good gracious, aren't you dressed yet?' she cried. 'Time's getting on, you know. Be quick now. I'll come and help you.'

Mary Kate hurried back to her bedroom without putting the top on the toothpaste and pulled open her sock drawer. She was half hoping her vest might be in there, but it wasn't.

'Where's your vest?' Mummy said, all ready to help Mary Kate to get dressed.

'Don't know,' mumbled Mary Kate, sitting on the edge of the bed to put on her clean socks.

Mummy pulled the bedclothes this way and that, looked under the bed, looked on the chair and behind the chair and in the wardrobe and then went across to the bathroom.

'It's not there,' called Mary Kate. 'I've looked.'

'I'm getting you a clean one,' Mummy said, coming

back with it. 'There's no time to mess about. You'll be late for school.'

She bundled Mary Kate into her clothes and then started to brush her hair. It was very tangly.

'Whatever were you doing last night?' asked Mummy. 'Your hair's like a bird's nest.'

Mary Kate said nothing. She thought she had better not tell Mummy she had been trying to make her hair into a pigtail, like her best friend Susan's.

Daddy had cleaned Mary Kate's shoes when he cleaned his. They were in the kitchen. Mary Kate ran down and put them on. She was in the hall, wriggling herself into her blazer, when she remembered she had promised Teddy she would take him to school with her today.

She rushed upstairs to fetch him.

'Where are you going NOW?' called Mummy, hearing her thump across the landing. 'You'll miss the bus if you're not quick.'

'I'm getting Teddy,' shouted Mary Kate, burrowing into the tangle of bedclothes at the bottom of the bed to find him.

Teddy was still in his pyjamas. They were very nice pyjamas. Auntie Mary had made them for him when he went to hospital with Mary Kate. All the same, he couldn't go to school in them. Mary Kate would have to dress him.

She unbuttoned his pyjama jacket. Then she stopped. Under his pyjamas Teddy was wearing Mary Kate's yesterday's vest.

'COME DOWNSTAIRS!' shouted Mummy from the hall. She sounded cross.

'Coming,' called Mary Kate and hastily pushed Teddy to the back of the toy cupboard, vest and all.

Mummy had the front door open, all ready to take Mary Kate up the hill to the bus stop, but they were hardly out of the house when the school bus went by.

'There!' cried Mummy. 'I said you'd miss it, didn't I?'

'I can go the field way, can't I?' said Mary Kate. 'It isn't raining.' When it rained the field path was muddy, especially the bit by the stream.

'You'll have to go by yourself, then,' Mummy told her. 'I can't come with you. I'm expecting the chimney sweep at a quarter to nine.'

All the same, Mummy went with her down the garden to the gate that led into the little wood.

'I'll come as far as the stile,' she said.

When they reached the stile, Mary Kate climbed

over, held up her face for a kiss and skipped away
across the field.

Mummy stood watching her for a moment, then
hurried back to the house. She must have been thinking very hard about something, because she quite forgot to shut the garden gate.

Jacky, the dog, dashed out of the kitchen as soon as
Mummy opened the back door. She didn't bother to
call him back. She thought he was quite safe, in the
garden.

It didn't take Jacky long to find the open gate. Tail

wagging, he trotted into the wood, sniffing at the narrow footpath.

Mary Kate had stopped on the bridge, to wait for the
ducks. They had all the time in the world, so they didn't
hurry themselves. She opened her satchel and took out
her packet of mid-morning biscuits. She had just
broken one up for the ducks when she heard Jacky
barking. He was racing across the field towards her.

Mary Kate knew it would be no use telling Jacky to
go home. He wouldn't take any notice of her. She
dropped the bits of biscuit into the stream and ran as
fast as she could towards the kissing-gate on the other
side of the field. Once she was in the churchyard,
Jacky couldn't follow her.

By the time Mary Kate reached the tall gate in the
churchyard wall, Jacky had squeezed under the kissing-
gate and was on the footpath behind her.

Panting, Mary Kate stretched up and wiggled hard
at the difficult latch. In another moment she was safe in
the churchyard. She was only just in time. Jacky
reached the gate as she slammed it shut. He pushed his
little black nose through the bars and whimpered.
Then he leapt up at the latch and began to bark.

Mary Kate could still hear him barking when she
ran into the school playground. She heard him several

times during the first part of the morning. Then he stopped. 'He's gone home,' she thought and by midday she had forgotten all about him.

She was washing her hands before school dinner when Susan dashed into the cloakroom. 'Your dog's in the playground,' she said. 'Come and see.'

Out ran Mary Kate – and there was Jacky, being petted and patted by a crowd of giggling children.

He had somehow found his way round to the street and in at the school gate. There was a barrier to stop the children running out into the road, but it couldn't stop Jacky.

As soon as he saw Mary Kate, he rushed at her, barking joyfully.

'You bad dog,' she said, catching him by the collar and trying to make him keep still.

'Is that your dog, Mary Kate?' asked Miss Laurie, coming to see what all the noise was.

'Yes, Miss Laurie,' said Mary Kate. 'He followed me to school this morning.'

'Well, you'd better send him home again,' Miss Laurie said. 'Put him out of the back gate. We don't want him loose in the street, do we?'

'No, Miss Laurie,' said Mary Kate meekly, and led the struggling Jacky across the playground to the back

gate. It was a rather rickety old gate and nobody used it now. The path behind it was quite overgrown and full of stinging nettles.

Mary Kate didn't want to push Jacky out on to the

weedy path, but Miss Laurie was watching her so there was nothing else she could do.

'Go on, go home,' she said, hoping he would find a hole in the hedge so that he could get into the field beyond.

Jacky whined and barked and jumped up at the gate as Mary Kate ran back across the playground to have her dinner.

Half-way through the meal, the children at the table near the door began to nudge one another and giggle. Some of them bent down and looked under the table.

Jacky had found his way back into the playground. Now he was in the dining-room, creeping along under the table, looking for Mary Kate.

The children patted his head and fed him with scraps from their plates, keeping one eye on Miss Laurie, who seemed not to have noticed that anything was going on. She was talking to the Dinner Lady and only half watching the children.

Suddenly Jacky found Mary Kate. He tried to get up on to her lap.

'What's happening?' cried Miss Laurie, coming to see. When she saw, she said, 'Oh, it's that dog again, is it? Well, if he won't go away I'm afraid he'll have to be tied up in the boiler house till it's time to go home.'

'Can't Mary Kate take him home?' asked Susan. 'I could go with her. It won't take us long.'

'Certainly not,' said Miss Laurie. 'I can't possibly allow you to go wandering off like that. You're in my charge till going-home time. I'm supposed to keep an eye on you and see you come to no harm.'

She took Jacky firmly by the collar and marched him off towards the boiler house.

Suddenly Mary Kate had an idea. 'Miss Laurie! Miss Laurie!' she shouted, running after her teacher.

'Can I take Jacky to Granny's?' she asked, pointing across the street to the lane where Granny lived. 'You can see her house from the corner of the playground. You'll be able to keep your eye on us.'

Granny *was* surprised when she opened her front door and found Mary Kate and Jacky standing there.

'Whatever next!' she said, when Mary Kate had explained. 'Off you go, now, before you get into any more trouble. I'll take Jacky home this afternoon. Let's hope Mummy hasn't been hunting for him all morning.'

Mary Kate went thoughtfully back to school. She had a feeling she *was* going to get into more trouble. Even if Mummy hadn't been hunting for Jacky, she had almost certainly been hunting for Mary Kate's yesterday's vest, which Teddy was still wearing.

A WALK AND AUNT MARY

AUNT MARY had come for the week-end. She had arrived on Friday afternoon, just in time to meet Mary Kate from school. Granny was there, too, so Mary Kate walked home the field way with them instead of going on the school bus.

Aunt Mary couldn't stay with Granny when she came to the village because the room she and Mummy shared when they were girls had been turned into a bathroom. The attic was Uncle Jack's room, just as it had been when he and Uncle Ned were boys.

Aunt Mary had a little room in Mary Kate's house. It opened off the dining-room and it had a glass door that led to the path by the side gate, so Aunt Mary could come and go as she pleased.

On Saturday morning Mary Kate and Aunt Mary did all the shopping. They walked to the village and did Mummy's shopping first. Then they called on Granny. They left Mummy's basket in Granny's kitchen while they did Granny's shopping. Aunt Mary said she thought they had earned themselves a special treat, so she took Mary Kate to the Bun Shop for coffee and cakes. Mary Kate's coffee was mostly milk but that was the way she liked it. She had a lovely, squashy, sugary fresh cream doughnut with it. The sugar stuck to her fingers and her face and a blob of cream somehow put itself on the end of her nose, so Aunt Mary had to clean her up with a paper napkin.

'There!' she said, when Mary Kate was more or less clean again. 'Now we'll take Granny her shopping and collect Mummy's and then we'll go home on the bus. I think we've done enough walking for one morning.'

'Don't you like walking?' asked Mary Kate.

'Some kinds of walking,' said Aunt Mary, 'but not trudging about with heavy shopping baskets.'

After lunch Mummy and Aunt Mary sat in the garden for a while and Mary Kate helped Daddy weed the flower border. Then they all tidied themselves and walked across the fields to have tea with Granny.

After tea Granny lit a fire because the evenings were still chilly and Mary Kate sat on Granny's rocking chair and rocked herself. She rocked and rocked and rocked and then she was asleep.

Mummy woke her up at last and said it was nearly time to go home.

'You shouldn't have let her sleep so long,' Granny said. 'She'll be awake half the night.'

By the time they had had supper and walked home the long way round because the field way was too dark, Mary Kate was quite tired again. It was much later than her usual bedtime. She went to sleep almost at once but she woke up very early on Sunday morning. The room was still dark but Mary Kate felt very wide awake, so she thought it must be time to get up. She slid out of bed and pulled back the curtains. It wasn't quite light yet, but all the birds were singing, whistling and trilling, wild and sweet and shrill, in the wood at the bottom of the garden.

'I'm terribly thirsty,' said Mary Kate, to no one in particular. Then she remembered it was Sunday and breakfast wouldn't be for a long time yet. She decided to creep downstairs and get herself a drink of water.

What a surprise she had when she opened the kitchen door! There was Aunt Mary, with her outdoor things on, standing by the draining board drinking a cup of tea.

'Good gracious me!' she said, when she saw Mary Kate. 'You're an early bird. Nearly as early as the ones that woke me up.'

'I want a drink,' Mary Kate said. 'Is it morning or is it still last night?'

'Morning,' Aunt Mary told her, 'but only just. Here, have a cup of tea.'

'Why have you got your coat on?' asked Mary Kate, curling her hands round the warm mug and sipping the sweet milky tea.

'I'm going for a walk,' said Aunt Mary. 'I'm going out to see the day begin. We don't get mornings like this in London – at least, not in the part of London where I live.'

Mary Kate drank her tea fast. 'Can I come with you?' she gasped, after the last mouthful.

Aunt Mary looked doubtful. Then she said, 'Well, I don't see why not. You're wide awake now so you probably won't go to sleep even if I send you back to bed. I'll go up and fetch your things. No need to wake Mummy and Daddy. Just give your hands and face a quick splash under the tap. You can have a proper wash when we come back.'

By the time Mary Kate had pretended to wash her face and hands, Aunt Mary was downstairs again with her clothes and her hairbrush. She dressed her quickly, smoothed her hair a bit and put her hat on.

Pussy Pipkin stirred in his basket by the stove,

stretched his long front legs, tipped back his head and yawned, licked down his front once, twice — and curled up again for more sleep.

'Where's Jacky?' asked Mary Kate, suddenly realizing he wasn't there.

'Asleep on the bottom of my bed,' said Aunt Mary. 'He thinks I didn't see him sneak in when I came out to put the kettle on.'

'Are we taking him with us? He's not supposed to sleep on beds,' Mary Kate said.

'I know he isn't,' said Aunt Mary, unlocking the back door, 'but I think we'll leave him there, and go

out this way. If we take him out he's sure to start barking and I don't think anybody wants to be woken up by a barking dog at half-past three on a Sunday morning.'

'Is that what time it is?' said Mary Kate, stepping out into the cool morning that hadn't quite started. 'It isn't *nearly* time to get up yet, is it?'

'Not for some people,' said Aunt Mary, 'but it's nearly time for the sun to get up and if we don't hurry we'll miss it.'

She led the way quickly down the garden, through the gate at the bottom and into the little wood. Mary

Kate hurried after her. It was creepy dark in the wood. Mary Kate caught hold of the back of Aunt Mary's coat as they went along the narrow path towards the stile.

Once they were in the field, it was lighter.

'Quick,' said Aunt Mary. 'The sky's getting pink already.'

They didn't take the path across the field to the churchyard. Instead, they climbed the sloping ground close to the wood till they reached the top of the hill.

There they stopped, to watch the sun come up. Pink and gold and glowing, burning bright with a splendid light, the day began. Mary Kate thought it was wonderful. She held Aunt Mary's hand and never said a word. Even the birds had hushed their morning noise for this marvellous moment. The sky changed from pale grey to blue and the fiery sun shone straight at Mary Kate, putting pink in her face.

'It's warm,' she said, blinking in the brilliant light. 'I can feel it warm already.'

'It's going to be a lovely day,' Aunt Mary said. 'Come on. Race you down the hill.'

They ran down the other side of the hill through the soaking grass. Now Mary Kate knew why Aunt Mary had told her to put her boots on and not her shoes.

Aunt Mary had a funny bag thing hanging from a strap over her shoulder. It was very old and rather shabby. It bumped up and down as she ran, so she pulled it round and held it under her arm.

She slowed down half-way down the hill and pretended to be quite worn out. Mary Kate reached the far fence first and leaned against it, waiting for Aunt Mary.

'What have you got in that bag?' she asked, breathlessly.

'Things,' said Aunt Mary. 'Two minutes' rest and then we'll go on round by Dingley Wood.'

They didn't go into the wood because it was cool with shadows and Aunt Mary wanted to stay out in the sunlight. They followed the field path all the way along by the chestnut paling fence and peered through the green gloom of the rhododendrons at the dark lines of pine trees beyond.

At the edge of the plantation, the trees were different. This was the old Dingley Wood, or what was left of it. Between the silver birches the ground was misty mauve with bluebells, and rabbit paths criss-crossed the tangled grasses.

'I'm hungry,' said Aunt Mary. 'How about you?'

'*Starving*,' said Mary Kate, but she didn't really want to go home yet, for breakfast.

'Let's go and sit on that tree-trunk,' suggested Aunt Mary, leading the way into the wood.

The fallen tree-trunk looked like a creature, with its broken leggy branches and sticking-up short snout.

Mary Kate pretended it was a monster and climbed on to its back.

Aunt Mary sat down and opened the knapsack she had been carrying.

'We'll have our picnic now,' she said.

Mary Kate was delighted. It was the first time she had had a picnic breakfast. Aunt Mary had brought a flask of tea, two crusty buttery rolls, three cold sausages, two tomatoes and a bar of chocolate. Mary Kate thought it was quite the nicest breakfast she had ever had.

When they had finished they picked a bunch of primroses to take home to Mummy.

'Shall we take some bluebells?' asked Mary Kate.

'Only one,' said Aunt Mary. 'Just to prove we've been here. Bluebells don't do very well indoors. They don't look right in a vase and they don't live long. They're better left where they are.'

'They don't smell the same indoors, do they?' said

Mary Kate, sniffing the delicately scented air. 'They smell lovely out here.'

'That's because there are so many of them here,' Aunt Mary told her.

The church clock struck six as they walked down the rutted cart track towards the lane that led back to the village.

'Mummy won't be up yet, will she?' asked Mary Kate. It felt very odd to be out in the fields while everyone else was in bed. She thought how surprised Mummy would be when she woke up and found no Mary Kate and no Aunt Mary in the house.

'Mummy won't be up for ages,' Aunt Mary said, 'but I expect Granny will. Shall we go and see?'

Granny *was* up. She was making herself a pot of tea when Aunt Mary and Mary Kate peeped through her kitchen window about half an hour later.

'Good gracious me!' she said, opening the door to let them in. 'Have you been out all night?'

'Not quite,' said Aunt Mary. 'We got up to see the sun rise. We just popped in for a cup of tea.'

'You might as well stay to breakfast now you're here,' said Granny.

'We've had our breakfast,' said Mary Kate. 'We had it in Dingley Wood.'

She drank her tea and then wandered off into Granny's parlour. Last night's fire was still alight, a heap of hot grey ashes, with here and there a glowing scrap of coal.

Mary Kate climbed into the rocking chair and began slowly to rock herself to and fro. When Aunt Mary looked in a few minutes later, she was curled up, fast asleep.

THE SCHOOL SPORTS

SPORTS DAY had come at last. For weeks Mary Kate had been practising for the egg-and-spoon race with a big spoon and a little potato. She was really quite good at it now.

She had been practising for the flat race, too. Mummy and Daddy had run races with her in the garden. They couldn't help her with the three-legged race, though. Mummy did try, once, just for fun. She and Mary Kate staggered all hunched up and hobble-de-hee across the lawn and fell in a heap on the grass.

'There's going to be an obstacle race,' Mary Kate said, at breakfast on the great day. 'You have to pick up a lot of rings and put them in a basket and dress up in a coat inside out and gloves and a hat and big Wellingtons and crawl through a barrel. I don't think I'll go in for that one. I'm sure I shall get all muddled up.'

'It won't matter,' Daddy said. 'It's only a bit of fun. I should have a go, if I were you.'

'Are you coming, Daddy?' asked Mary Kate. 'Mummy's coming. So is Granny. Lots of daddies are coming.'

'I'll do my best,' Daddy promised. 'It all depends how much work I find waiting for me when I get to the office. If I can possibly get away, I will. I can't be sure I'll be there at the start, but I'll do my best to come before it's all over. Anyway, good luck, poppet.'

He gave Mary Kate a quick kiss and went off to catch his train.

'I hope he can come,' Mary Kate said.

'Well, it *is* Friday,' said Mummy, 'so he's much more likely to be able to get away today than any other day. Anyway, I'll be there to cheer you on. Look out for me right at the start.'

It wasn't easy to settle down to proper lessons that morning. Even the teachers kept looking out of the window to make sure the sun was still shining. There were a lot of last-minute preparations still to be made and everyone was so busy that Miss Laurie quite forgot to blow the whistle after mid-morning break, so there was a longer playtime than usual.

While the children were having their dinners, the parents who had offered to help came to take the chairs

71

and benches from the school to the Sports Field. There were several cars with roof-racks, three small vans, a tractor and trailer and Mr Bean, with his horse and cart. Mr Bean always closed his junk-yard and his second-hand shop on Sports Day and came to help at the school.

It wasn't long before the benches had been taken out of the school hall and the store room and the chairs out of the classrooms. Then the fun began. As the children finished their dinners, they carried their chairs out into the playground. Each child with a chair was greeted with a cheer from the children by the gate.

Mary Kate loved every minute of it. Most of the children had seen it all before, of course, but to her it was all new and exciting. She watched the cars and the vans drive away with the chairs, and the tractor move slowly off with its trailer-load of long benches. Mr Bean was the last to go.

His horse and cart followed the procession down the lane where Granny lived, past the little fenced-off Green where the swings were, to the Recreation

Ground, which was the cricket pitch and the football field and the place where the Fête was held.

At last the time came for the children to go to the Sports Field. They lined up in the playground in a long, long, wriggly crocodile, all wearing their blue shorts and white shirts and carrying their cardigans and pullovers.

Then two of the teachers held up the traffic and the crocodile hurried across the road and down the little lane on the other side. Mary Kate was right in the front, with Susan.

Just as the children reached Granny's cottage, her door opened and she came out.

'There's Granny!' cried Mary Kate, waving her hand. At that, all the other children waved, too. Granny stood at her gate and watched them. She was wearing her best hat and coat, all ready to come and see Mary Kate run in the races.

There were quite a lot of mothers and fathers in the field when the children arrived. Mary Kate looked to see if her Mummy was there, but she wasn't.

'I s'pose Granny's waiting for her,' she said, when Granny didn't appear. Mary Kate had expected her to follow the long line of children down the lane.

It was a lovely day. It hadn't rained for so long that

74

the ground was quite dry and warm. The children sat cross-legged on the short grass, because all the chairs and benches were needed for the parents and friends. The sky was so bright and the sun so hot that Mary Kate began to feel a little sleepy. She closed her eyes.

'There's my Mummy,' said Susan loudly – and woke her up.

It was almost time for the races to start. Miss Chesney was looking at her watch and Miss Laurie was looking at the list of children who were in the first race.

Mary Kate began to feel a little anxious. She screwed up her eyes and looked all round the field. There were the babies in their prams and the toddlers rolling about on the grass. There were the grannies and aunties and mothers, in their gay summer frocks and pretty hats. There were even a few fathers, in flannels and white shirts, with the sleeves rolled up. There was the man from the local paper, with his camera. There were two men in grey suits and panama hats. Mary Kate didn't know who they were. They were talking to the vicar. He was wearing his dark Sunday suit and he looked rather hot.

Miss Laurie blew her whistle. The children stopped chattering.

'First race. Under fives,' said a queer booming voice. It was one of the panama hat men. He was calling through a megaphone.

Mary Kate looked round the field again. She stared at all the smiling faces but the face she wanted to see wasn't there. *Her* Mummy hadn't come.

The next race was the flat race for the five-year-olds. This was Mary Kate's first race. She lined up with the other children, wondering what could have happened to Mummy and Granny.

'Don't look at the people, Mary Kate, or you'll run all crooked,' said Miss Laurie. 'Keep your eye on that big oak at the far end of the field.'

Mary Kate stared miserably at the oak tree. She stared at it so hard she didn't realize she was supposed to start running till she saw the others rush forward. She ran as fast as she could but she didn't win. She trailed across the field behind the others and went back to her place beside Susan.

'Your Gran's just come,' Susan said. 'She's over there. Look.'

Mary Kate looked. There was Granny, standing behind the second row of chairs, waving a scarf at her.

Mary Kate waved back and sat down. She still couldn't see Mummy anywhere but at least there would be somebody there belonging to her to see her run in the other races.

All the flat races were run first. It was a good arrangement because that way nobody had to run in two races straight off.

Then it was time for Mary Kate's egg-and-spoon race.

She felt much more nervous about this race than she had about the first one. Her hand shook as she stood at the starting line, holding the big metal spoon. The old, rough, wooden egg rolled about in the most alarming way. Mary Kate was sure she was going to drop it.

The other panama hat man was starting the races. He blew one blast on a whistle, very clear and shrill.

'Ready ... steady ... pee-ee-eep,' he went. Off went the children, walking stiffly, looking down at their spoons, trying not to wobble.

Mary Kate was doing very well. She was in third place. Out of the corner of her eye she could see the white line painted on the grass, so she knew she was going straight. She could see the heels of the two children in front, too, but she didn't know who they were.

The people were cheering and calling the children's names.

'Come on, Johnny . . . come on, Sally . . . come on, Susan . . .'

Then, suddenly, loudly, clearly, somebody shouted, 'Come on, Mary Kate!'

It was Daddy! It was Daddy, cheering her on, louder than anybody else. He had come, after all. He must have let Mummy know, somehow, and she had been waiting for him.

Mary Kate almost ran, she was so happy. The spoon jerked in her hand. The egg lurched sideways, tipped to the rim of the spoon, tottered – and rolled back into place. Mary Kate's heart was thumping and her throat was dry. She had almost dropped the egg.

There couldn't be far to go now but she didn't dare look up. There seemed to be no one else on the field – just herself, walking and walking and almost bursting with trying not to drop the precious egg.

All about her voices were calling and they all seemed to be saying the same thing.

'Come on, Mary Kate . . . come on, Mary Kate . . . Mary Kate . . . Mary Kate . . .'

Then it was over. She saw the tape – she touched it – she heard Miss Chesney's voice say, 'Well done, Mary Kate. My goodness, you *were* fast. It was most exciting.'

79

Mary Kate smiled and looked past Miss Chesney to the long line of mothers and fathers and aunties and grannies, all smiling and clapping. She was looking for her own Mummy and Daddy and Granny.

There they were, waving to her, hurrying along behind the chairs – Mummy and Daddy and Granny and Uncle Jack and Aunt Mary and Uncle Ned and Auntie Dot.

No wonder there had been so many voices cheering her on. The whole family had come with Daddy to see Mary Kate win her very first race.